Can't Have Ants

by Sarah Willson
illustrated by Steve Haefele

Simon Spotlight/Nickelodeon
New York   London   Toronto   Sydney   Singapore

Discovery Facts

Tamandua (tuh MAN doo uh): A type of anteater that lives in South America. It has long, curved nails and a long snout, both of which help it to root out ants. Tamanduas spend most of their lives in trees. Their favorite foods are ants, termites, and bees.

Three-toed sloth (slohth): a small mammal that probably got its name because it tends to move slowly and because it has three long claws on each of its feet. Its front legs are longer than its back legs. Three-toed sloths live mostly in trees and eat young leaves and tender twigs.

Cecropia tree (sih KRAH pee uh): A type of tree that grows in the rain forest. Cecropias grow very quickly, usually in clearings. Their trunks are hollow and their wood is often used by local people for floats.

Azteca ants (az TEK uh): A type of ant that lives in the hollow trunks of cecropia trees. The ants feed on special food at the base of each cecropia leaf. They protect the tree by viciously attacking anything that touches it.

Liana (lee AN uh): A woody vine that can climb as high as the tree canopy in a tropical forest. Sometimes two lianas may grow side by side, and the intertwining branches form a natural "ladder."

KLASKY CSUPO INC.

Based on the TV series *The Wild Thornberrys*® created by Klasky Csupo, Inc. as seen on Nickelodeon®

SIMON SPOTLIGHT
An imprint of Simon & Schuster Children's Publishing Division
1230 Avenue of the Americas, New York, New York 10020

86-19260

"Right-ho!" said Nigel Thornberry. "Are you quite ready to shoot some tip-top footage of the middle canopy, darling?"

"Girls," Marianne said firmly. "I want the Commvee com-PLETE-ly cleaned up by the time your father and I get back this afternoon."

"Sure Mom. And then we can go to the village tonight, right?" Debbie asked anxiously. "I know where to get a copy of *Teenage Wasteland* that's only three months old!"

Marianne looked stern. "If it's clean, we go. If it's not, we stay."

"Come along, poppet," called Nigel. "I do so want to capture footage of the tamandua and the rare three-toed sloth!" He and Marianne disappeared into the jungle foliage.

"C'mon, Darwin!" said Eliza to the chimpanzee. "Let's go see if *we* can find the tamandua!"

"Not so fast, Dweeb!" said Debbie. "You're forgetting that *tree* branch *you* left inside the Commvee! You better drag it out! I *have* to get to the village. If I don't get that new copy of *Teenage Wasteland* tonight, some other desperate teenager will snap it up. Then I will like, totally die."

"I promise I'll move my branch out as soon as I get back," said Eliza. "I'm going to carve a canoe from it."

Debbie grabbed Donnie by the hand and stormed into the Commvee.

"Eliza," said Darwin in a worried voice, "I do think we should stay and help clean up. We're critically low on Cheese Munchies. Your mother can stock up tonight at the village!"

Eliza rolled her eyes. "Aw, Darwin, forget your stomach just once. We'll do a quick search for the tamandua and the sloth. Then we'll come right back, I promise," she replied.

And off she stamped, toward the brush and the jungle beyond. With a sigh, Darwin followed. They hadn't gone more than a few steps when a bloodcurdling scream came from the Commvee.

Eliza and Darwin dashed back toward the Commvee. Debbie was staggering away from the vehicle. "EEEEE-LI-ZUHHHH!" she shrieked.

"What's the matter?" Eliza called.

"What's the *matter* is that there are man-eating *ants* inside our *house*! *That's* what's the matter!" bellowed Debbie. "All I did was *touch* that dumb branch of yours and they swarmed all over the place, including *me*! And those ants *bite,* too!"

"Oh," said Eliza sheepishly. "Sorry, Deb. I didn't know the ants were inside the branch. I'll find something to get rid of them."

"What, you think sticks and mud from the jungle are going to get rid of all those ants? They're *swarming* in there!"

"Be right back, promise!" Eliza called over her shoulder as she rushed away.

"You *better* be!" yelled Debbie.

"And now what, Eliza?" huffed Darwin, right behind her.

"We really have to find that tamandua now," said Eliza. "A tamandua s a kind of anteater! We can get the anteater to eat all the ants out of the Commvee. It's our only hope."

"I don't like this one bit," complained Darwin.

They found a sturdy liana and started climbing. "Psssst," whispered Eliza as she nudged Darwin. "That's a tamandua."

"Excuse me," she said to it. "But I wonder if you could help me? I know where there are a bunch of ants that built a nest in a cecropia branch. Could you, uh, come eat them for me?"

"Nope," the tamandua answered. "Those must be azteca ants. Too vicious for me. Never touch 'em."

"Oh," said Eliza in a small voice. "Darwin, *now* what am I going to do? Debbie is going to kill me."

Suddenly she and Darwin heard the tamandua mutter something. "What was that you said?" Eliza asked.

"Try him," repeated the tamandua, casually pointing higher in the tree. Eliza and Darwin looked up.

"It's a three-toed sloth!" exclaimed Eliza. "Thanks!" she said as she climbed higher into the tree.

"Hi," she greeted the sloth. "Do you like to eat azteca ants?"

"I do not eat ants," he said stiffly. "I eat only leaves and twigs."

"Oh," said Eliza. "There is no way I can get that cecropia branch out of the Commvee if no one will eat those ants," she said. "I am in big trouble, Darwin!"

"Wait! Did you say 'cecropia?'" asked the sloth, suddenly looking a bit more lively. "I *love* cecropia leaves!"

Eliza brightened. "Follow me!" she said.

As they crawled from one tree branch to another, they could hear Debbie ranting before the Commvee was even in sight.

Eliza directed the sloth toward the Commvee. He disappeared inside.

"Of all the sisters I could have gotten stuck with, I get Geekahontas, the boat maker!" Debbie was saying to no one in particular. "Oh, there you are! Did you find a nice bug zapper out there in the jungle?"

"Um, sort of," said Eliza. "First I just have to go check on something."

She walked around to the back of the Commvee.

"You're all set," said the sloth.

"You mean, the ants are all out of the Commvee?" asked Eliza incredulously.

"Yup," he said. "See, I don't eat the *ants.* I just dragged the branch outside to eat the *leaves,* and the ants came with it."

Eliza heaved a huge sigh of relief. "Thank you *so* much!" she exclaimed to the sloth.

The sloth nodded and creeped back toward where he had come from. Eliza ran to find Debbie.

"It's all set," she said.

Debbie's eyes narrowed. "What do you mean, 'it's all set'?"

"The ants are all gone," said Eliza. "Go ahead. See for yourself."

Debbie opened the door carefully and stepped inside. Eliza, Darwin, and Donnie followed her.

"I don't know what you did, bugs-for-brains, but you are so lucky they're gone," said Debbie. "Now hurry up and help me clean before Mom and Dad get back."

They had just finished the last of the dusting when Nigel and
Marianne trudged into the clearing, weary and disappointed.

"So sorry, poppets," said Nigel, "but it looks like we have
to stay in the jungle another day. We got no footage whatsoever."

"But the Commvee is clean!" wailed Debbie. "What about my
magazine?"

"I know, honey," said Marianne soothingly. "Maybe just
another day or so. We need to get that footage and tamanduas
and sloths are so hard to find."

"Be right back!" yelled Eliza, scampering off.

"Excuse me again!" said Eliza, poking her head through the leaves and addressing the tamandua and the sloth. "But would you mind too much if my mom and dad took some footage of you? You don't have to stop eating at all."

The tamandua shrugged indifferently. The sloth nodded sleepily. "Thanks!" yelled Eliza, as she climbed down to tell her parents.

"I don't know how you ever spotted them, darling!" said Marianne
a little later as she packed away the last of her equipment. "But I sure
am glad you did!"

"Yes, biscuit, that was rippingly good naturalist work!" beamed Nigel.
Eliza smiled. Debbie rolled her eyes.

"And I'm *so* proud of you girls and how you worked together to clean up the Commvee!" said Marianne to her daughters as she hopped behind the wheel and revved the engine. "Let's go to the village!"

Debbie shouted, "*Teenage Wasteland*, here I come!"

"Mom, I think we need some more Cheese Munchies, too," said Eliza winking at Darwin.

"Okay, honey," said Marianne. "And girls, from now on let's try to keep the Commvee clean. We don't want to attract ants."